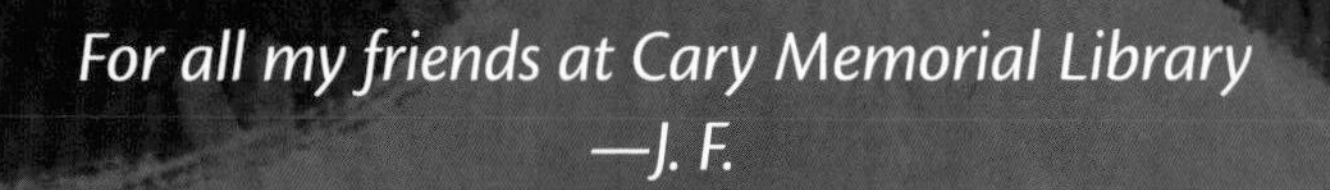
For all my friends at Cary Memorial Library
—J. F.

To Jamey and my three dogs: Samurai, Hansel, and Jinx
—E. T.

Published by Two Lions, New York

www.apub.com

ISBN-13: 9781542045650 (hardcover)
ISBN-10: 1542045657 (hardcover)

The illustrations are rendered in digital media.

Book design by AndWorld Design
Printed in China

First Edition
10 9 8 7 6 5 4 3 2 1

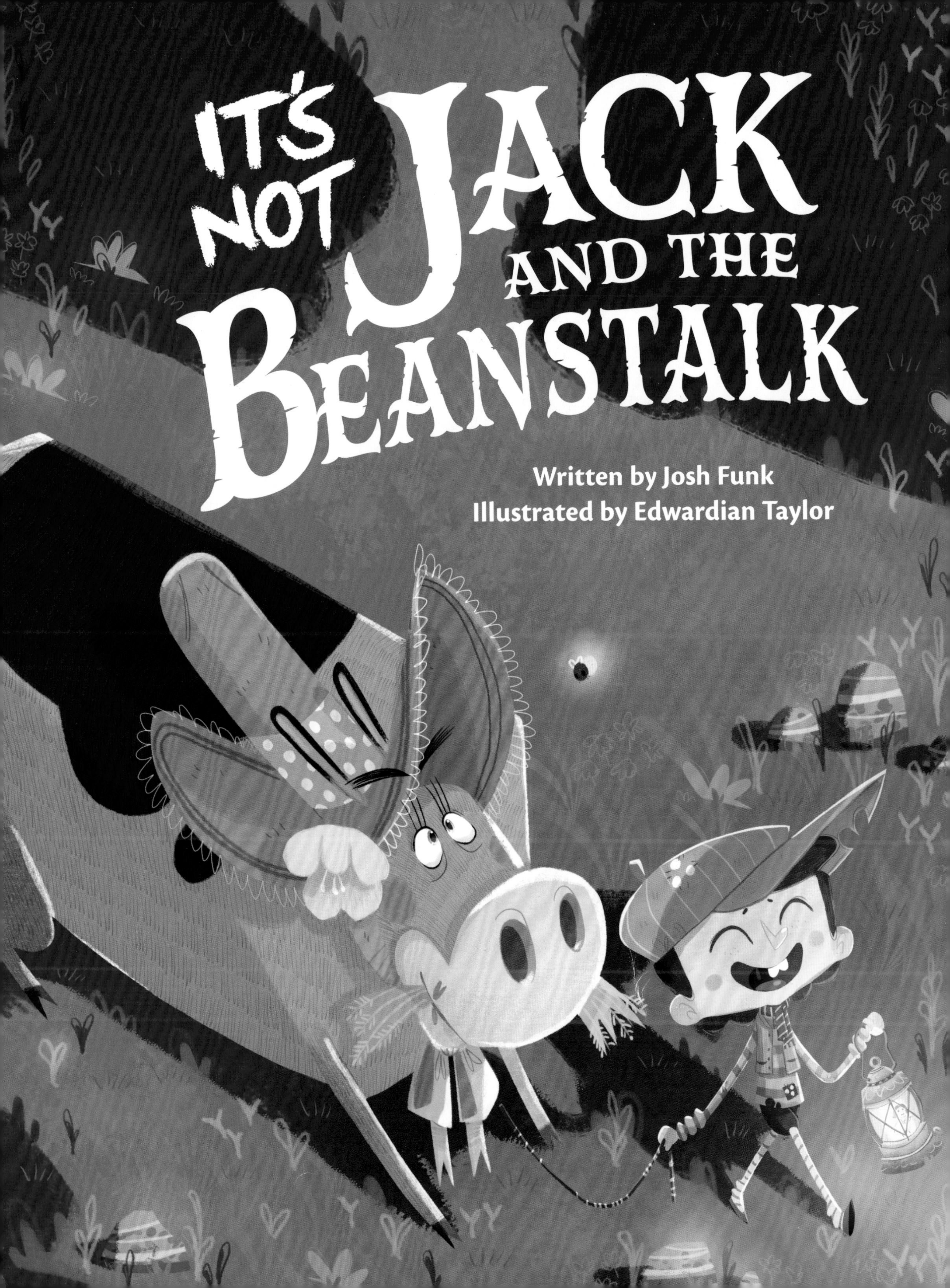

IT'S NOT JACK AND THE BEANSTALK

Written by Josh Funk
Illustrated by Edwardian Taylor

Once upon a time, Jack lived in a tiny cottage in a dreary village. He always dreamed that someday he would find his fortune.

And put on some pants!

Jack had no possessions other than a single cow. Unfortunately, the cow stopped giving milk, so Jack took her to the village market to sell her.

I didn't WRITE the story, Jack. I'm just telling it.
I'm so sorry, Bessie Cowpoke McPinwheel!

Jack was offered five beans in exchange for his cow.
Five beans? That stinks! And beans make me toot.
Jack, they're magic beans.
MAGIC? Will they grant wishes? I wish I had my cow back!

Jack tried to figure out how to make the magic beans work.

Jack grew so frustrated and angry that he threw the beans out the window.

NO!
I said: Jack grew so frustrated and angry that he threw the beans out the window.
And then he went to bed!
Aww, but I'm not tired. This story keeps getting worse and worse.

Jack woke the next morning to find that an enormous beanstalk had grown right where the magic beans had landed.
Whoa! It's a good thing I didn't eat those beans!
Jack began climbing up the beanstalk.
You're joking, right?

No, Jack,
you HAVE to climb the beanstalk.
Yikes. Can I at least grab my climbing gear?
NO!
I said you had no possessions!
ARGH! Will you make it shorter then? I'm not climbing it unless you change the size!
Fine!

SERIOUSLY?

Jack climbed for hours and began to grow tired.
I'm not SO tired. All that cow's milk over the years made me strong.
Despite being **soooo incredibly** tired, Jack climbed on.
I think I can see Cinderella's castle!

HEY, CINDY!
JACK? WHAT ARE YOU DOING?
IT'S KIND OF A LONG STORY.
CAN YOU TELL ME TONIGHT?
I'M HOSTING A BALL AT MY PALACE.
LET ME CHECK.
Hey, is this story going to end soon? Cindy invited me to a ball.
Stop TALKING and keep CLIMBING!
But she throws the BEST parties!

When Jack arrived at the top of the beanstalk, he found himself in front of a humongous house.
I'll bet a giant lives there.
Jack entered the house.
Are you sure about that?
Yes! Jack definitely entered the house.

Everything inside the house
was tremendously large.
Spoiler alert: A giant lives here. Can I go home now?
Suddenly, Jack heard
a booming voice—
FEE-FI-FO-FUM, I SMELL THE BLOOD OF AN ENGLISHMAN.
Umm, that doesn't even rhyme. How about: Fee-fi-fo-fum, I can see the giant's bum?

ARE YOU MAKING FUN OF ME?
No, I was only trying to help you rhyme better. Plus, technically, I'm from Scotland.
Would you please stop chit-chatting! I'm telling a story here!
Fine, Mr. Crankypants.

The giant noticed that Jack was stealing his bag of gold coins, his goose that laid golden eggs, and his magic harp.

Jack had finally found his fortune.
But before he could get away with it . . .

. . . the giant snatched him up.
AHHH! Let me go!
I knew I never should have climbed that beanstalk.

The giant carried Jack to the kitchen.

You know, there's a good chance that you're gonna die at the end of this story.
REALLY? IS THAT TRUE?
Jack, shush!
Don't tell him that!
Let's just . . . continue the story.
The giant—
I DON'T WANT TO DIE.
Neither do I! Do you have to eat me?
ACTUALLY, I'M A VEGAN.

ENOUGH!!!

GIANT! YOU'RE SUPPOSED TO ACCIDENTALLY SET JACK FREE AND CHASE HIM DOWN THE BEANSTALK!

JACK! YOU'RE SUPPOSED TO GET YOUR AX AND CHOP DOWN THE BEANSTALK!

HEY, ARE YOU HUNGRY?
Yes, Fred. I haven't eaten since this story started. It's been all climb this beanstalk and steal that gold.
THIS IS NOT HOW THE STORY IS SUPPOSED TO GO.
I HAVE A DELICIOUS RECIPE FOR TACO SALAD.
Great! You can use some beans from the beanstalk outside.

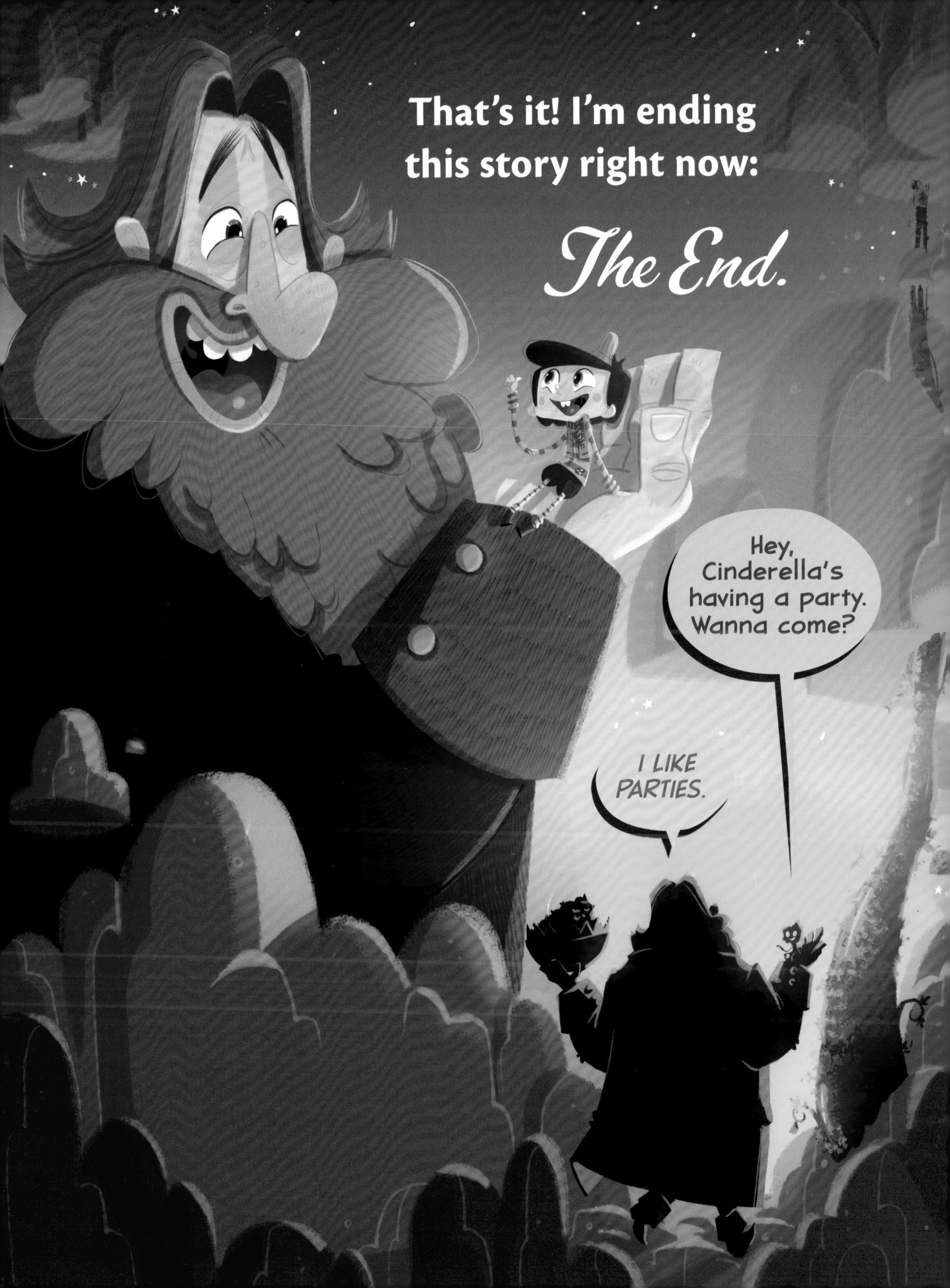
That's it! I'm ending this story right now:
The End.
Hey, Cinderella's having a party. Wanna come?
I LIKE PARTIES.

Thanks for coming to my party! This taco salad is delicious. How did you two meet?
NO! I already ended the story! There's no party!
THE END!
THE END!
THE END!
Well, I lived in a tiny cottage in a dreary village. I always dreamed that someday I would find my fortune.
Wait a minute! Those are MY lines! Telling the story is MY job!

And on our way here, Fred offered to share his fortune with me. We've decided to open a restaurant called "Where Have You Bean?"
WE'LL SERVE ONLY BEANS.

You've completely ruined everythi—

Oh, wait.

It all worked out?
I mean, it all worked out . . .
exactly as I'd planned.

And they all lived happily ever after.

JACK ALREADY SAID THAT.

Ugh. **The End.**

At least you finally got one thing right.

JACK
JACK